P9-CAL-669

SHANTY BOAT

SHANTY BOAT

CHARLES TEMPLE

Illustrated by MELANIE HALL

Houghton Mifflin Company
Boston 1994

WHETSTONE ELEMENTARY
LIBRARY

10/98 - Bookfair - $14.95 - #137

Text copyright © 1994 by Charles Temple
Illustrations copyright © 1994 by Melanie Hall

All rights reserved. For information about permission
to reproduce selections from this book, write to
Permissions, Houghton Mifflin Company, 215 Park Avenue
South, New York, New York 10003.

Library of Congress Cataloging-in-Publication Data

Temple, Charles A., 1947–
Shanty boat / by Charles Temple ; illustrated by Melanie Hall.
p. cm.
Summary: Relates the life of a happy river boatman who has since died but can still be seen on the river when the moon is bright.
ISBN 0-395-66163-3
[1. Boats and boating – Fiction. 2. Stories in rhyme.] I. Hall, Melanie, ill. II. Title.
PZ8.3.T2187Sh 1994 92-46025
[E] – dc20 CIP
AC

Printed in the United States of America

BP 10 9 8 7 6 5 4 3 2 1

To my mother, for poems,
and to my father, for boats.
– C.T.

To the memory of my father,
Edward A. Winsten, M.D.
– M.H.

My Uncle Sheb never milked him a cow,
Goin' down, down, ever downstream.
My Uncle Sheb never milked him a cow,
Nor dug him a garden, nor steered him a plow,
Nor plucked him a chicken, nor slopped him a sow,
Goin' down, down, ever downstream.

My Uncle Sheb never took him a wife,
Goin' down, down, ever downstream.
My Uncle Sheb never took him a wife
'Cause the women see him coming gonna run for their life,
Or skedaddle him away with a skillet or a knife,
Goin' down, down, ever downstream.

Uncle Sheb lived on a shanty boat,
Goin' down, down, ever downstream.
Uncle Sheb lived on a shanty boat.
They called it the shabbiest thing afloat –
"Looks more like a home for a pig or a goat."
Goin' down, down, ever downstream.

Weren't a thing in the world but a cabin on a raft,
Goin' down, down, ever downstream.
Weren't a thing in the world but a cabin on a raft
With a couple of cane poles, fore and aft.
And the sooner folks saw it, then the sooner folks laughed,
Goin' down, down, ever downstream.

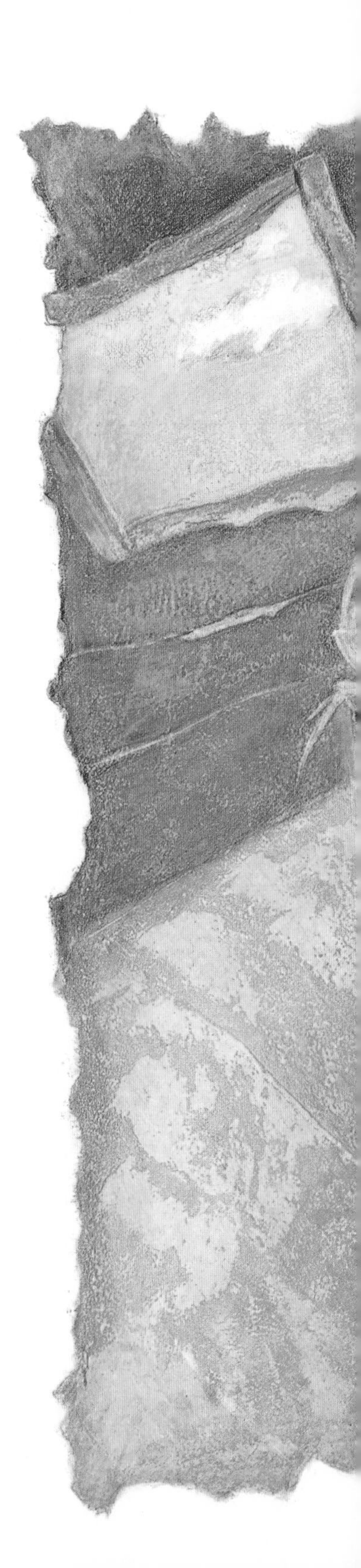

Still, it made Uncle Sheb a happy man,
Goin' down, down, ever downstream.
Still, it made Uncle Sheb a happy man
With the wood coals glowin' in an old paint can
And a catfish sizzlin' in the frying pan,
Goin' down, down, ever downstream.

Sippin' sassafras tea from an old fruit jar,
Goin' down, down, ever downstream.
Sippin' sassafras tea from an old fruit jar
Till he kicked right back to watch a star.
He couldn't go fast, but he sure went far,
Goin' down, down, ever downstream.

From Saint Louis, Mo, to the French bayou,
Goin' down, down, ever downstream.
From Saint Louis, Mo, to the French bayou,
Past Cairo and Cape Girardoo,
He'd fish and pole and fuss and chew,
Goin' down, down, ever downstream.

St. Louis
ILLINOIS
MISSOURI
Cape Girardeau
Cairo
TENNESSEE
ARKANSAS
LOUISIANA
MISSISSIPPI
New Orleans
GULF OF MEXICO

About the only thing that could give him a fright –
Goin' down, down, ever downstream.
About the only thing that could give him a fright
Was to hang up on a snag in the middle of the night –
Had to chop himself loose by the pale moonlight,
Goin' down, down, ever downstream.

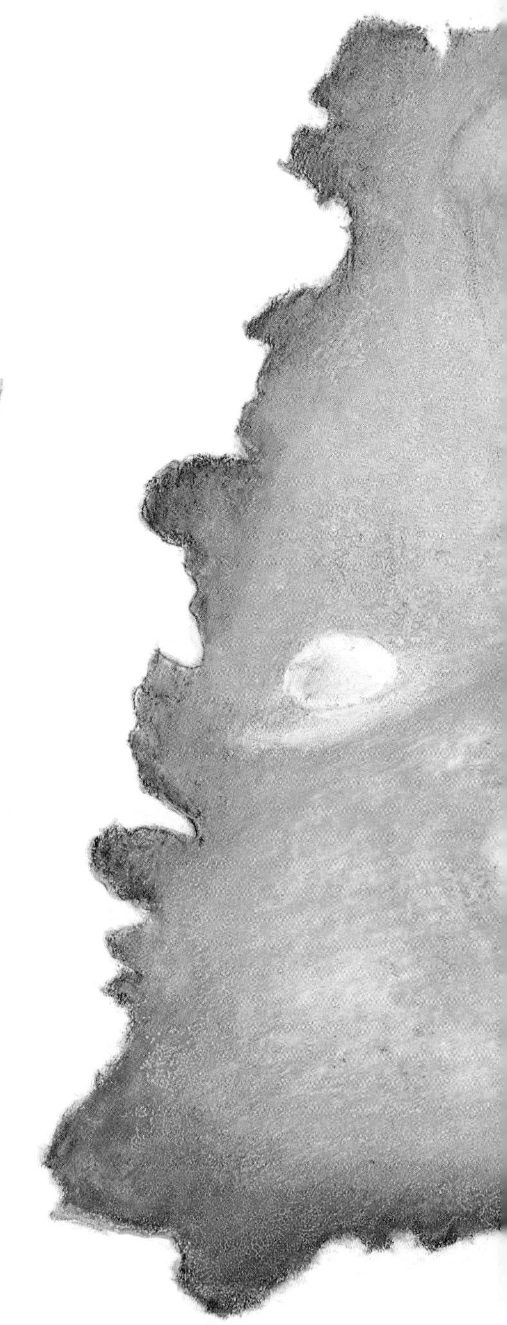

Uncle Sheb up 'n' died last fall,
Goin' down, down, ever downstream.
Uncle Sheb up 'n' died last fall,
So they piled on bricks and cannonball
And they sank that shanty boat, uncle and all,
Goin' down, down, ever downstream.

They say on the river when the moon is bright,
Goin' down, down, ever downstream.
They say on the river when the moon is bright,
If you watch and squint your eyes just right,
You'll see a shanty boat passin' in the middle of the night,
Goin' down, down, ever downstream.

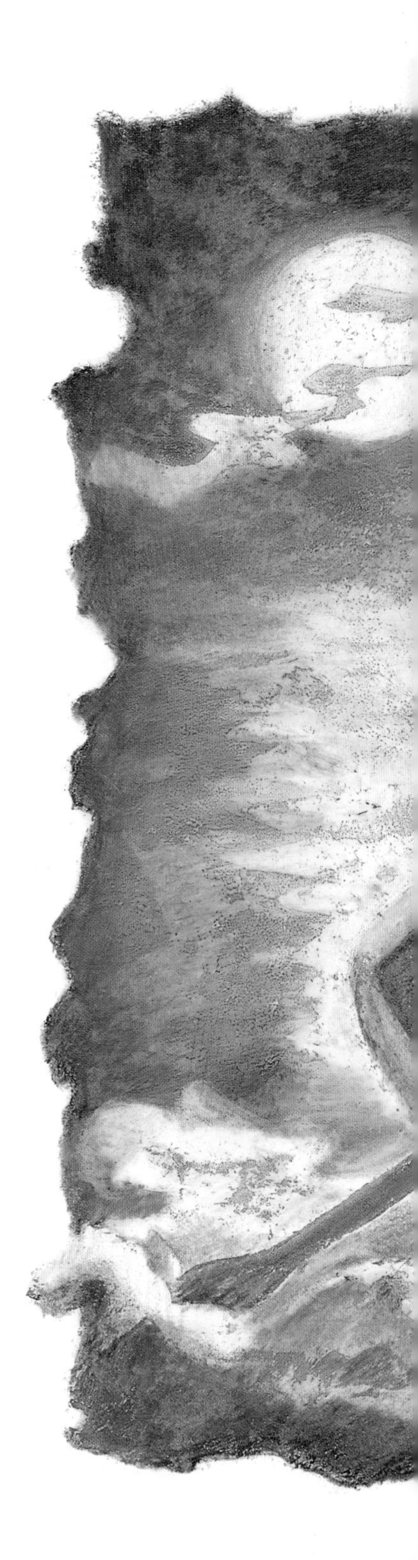

With an old man standin' by the steering oar,
Goin' down, down, ever downstream.
With an old man standin' by the steering oar,
Guess it *could* be Sheb, but you can't be sure.
Still, I like to think he's back for more,
Goin' down, down, ever downstream.

Uncle Sheb lived on a shanty boat,
Goin' down, down, ever downstream.
Uncle Sheb lived on a shanty boat.
They called it the shabbiest thing afloat –
"Looks more like a home for a pig or a goat."
Goin' down, down, ever downstream,

Goin' down, down, ever downstream.

WITHDRAWN